Secrets of Shiloh

By

Jill Watson Glassco

Illustrated by Donny Finley

Secrets of Shiloh

All quoted Scriptures and paraphrased passages are taken from the NEW AMERICAN STANDARD BIBLE© Copyright © 1960, 1962, 1963, 1968, 1971, 1972, 1973, 1975, 1977, 1995 by The Lockman Foundation. Used by permission.

WestBow Press books may be ordered through booksellers or by contacting:

WestBow Press
A Division of Thomas Nelson
1663 Liberty Drive
Bloomington, IN 47403
www.westbowpress.com
1-(866) 928-1240

ISBN: 978-1-4908-0350-0 (sc)
ISBN: 978-1-4908-0351-7 (e)

Library of Congress Control Number: 2013913780

Printed in the United States of America.

WestBow Press rev. date: 7/30/2013

WestBow
PRESS
A DIVISION OF THOMAS NELSON

To my two heroes:

My Lord Jesus, the Promise-Keeper

Not one of Your good promises failed; all have come to pass!

and

Phillip, my superman! I treasure your

faithful love, wisdom, knowledge, strength, endless patience, and encouraging support!

Contents

Chapter 1:
The Letter

Rachel hesitated for a moment and then lifted the rusty latch. The hinges moaned in protest as the heavy gates slowly swung open. For the first time in months, the sixteen-year-old stepped through the entrance of Shiloh and walked toward the antebellum house.

A sharp February wind rocked the branches of the enormous oak trees standing at attention along both sides of the long driveway. The once manicured grounds now lay hidden under a cover of brown leaves and tall weeds.

Thick ivy clinging to the brick foundation of the old home climbed past the third story to a gabled roof. Cracks zigzagged between the weathered stones of the front steps, and whitewash paint peeled from the oversized columns.

Rachel pulled a crumpled letter from a pocket of her jeans and sat down on the cold steps. Tears streamed down her cheeks and dripped off her chin onto her cardigan, which provided less-than-adequate protection from the winter chill, as she twirled the gold key on the necklace the Colonel had given her the last time she saw him.

"You promised the Lord would take care of me, that He would chase after me with His goodness," she cried. "Well, Col. James, where *is* His goodness? Tell me why *nothin'* has gotten *any* better since you left; in fact, everything's worse! Everybody at school's lookin' at colleges, but there's no way Mama can afford for me to go. It takes all we make in her two jobs and my babysittin' just to pay our bills."

She jerked her jacket tighter across her chest and sobbed, "And I'm *still* wearing these old hand-me-downs from the thrift store. On top of that, your letter makes no sense to me at all! Why didn't you just tell me the answer to my problems? Why did you have to leave me, Col. James? At least life was fun when you were here. Why did you have to die? Is taking you away from me God's idea of goodness?"

Resting her chin on her knees, Rachel spread out the well-worn piece of paper on the step by her feet. For the hundredth time, she read:

Dear Rachel,

Don't be afraid, Little Lamb, for the Lord has seen your SOS and is chasing after you with His goodness. The answer to all your troubles rests at Shiloh. I promise!

With love from your friend,

Col. James

"That's my sweater" Mary Alice Wicker said loudly enough for all the children on the bus to hear. Pointing her finger at Rachel, she asked, "Where'd you get that old thing, Rachel – out of a *rag* bag?"

"Oh hush your mouth, Mary Alice," Martin countered and then looked toward the girl seated beside him. "Don't pay any attention to her, Rach. She's just jealous because that sweater looks so pretty on *you*."

Sixth graders Rachel Grant and Martin Fitzpatrick had been pals as long as they could both remember. When Rachel was two, she and her mother, Bethany, had moved into a house a couple of blocks away from the Fitzpatrick family. Wayne and Dianne Fitzpatrick often helped with repairs around the Grants' home and sometimes included Bethany and Rachel in family meals, even though they had five little mouths of their own to feed. Because Bethany worked as a receptionist at a doctor's office on weekdays and waited tables at a local restaurant three nights a week, Rachel had spent many days over the past nine years under the tender watch of Mrs. Fitzpatrick.

Rachel bolted from her seat as soon as the bus stopped. "See ya tomorrow, Marty," she called back over her shoulder. She knew that if she looked at her best friend, she wouldn't be able to hide her hurt feeling or hold back the hot tears stinging her blue eyes. Looking straight ahead, Rachel hurried past Mary Alice, exited the bus, and then ran toward home.

After the school bus rolled out of sight, Rachel slowed to a snail's pace and stopped at the towering iron gates baring the name: Shiloh. The Hamilton family had built this widespread cotton plantation in the 1800s before the Civil War. Col. James Beauregard Hamilton, a descendent of the original owners, moved to the fifteen-hundred-acre estate in 1981 after retiring from a long military career. Retaining a forty-acre tract and the mansion, the Colonel sold the remainder of the property to the small town of Ebenezer in South Alabama.

The ageing World War II veteran kept to himself most of the time. No one in Ebenezer knew much about him except that he had been "married" to the army and seemed to have no close friends or family. Bethany had served him once at the diner, but Rachel had never even laid eyes on the mysterious man living in isolation behind those impenetrable gates.

She dropped her schoolbooks on the sidewalk and peeped through the bars. Shiloh's grounds were breathtaking. Three-hundred-year-old, giant oaks extended their massive, moss-covered arms to provide a canopy over the driveway. An immaculately trimmed lawn accented with stunning flower gardens and ornate, cascading fountains surrounded the old manor.

"Man!" Rachel murmured. "I wish I was rich and didn't have any problems."

From behind the azalea bushes along the privacy wall, a man's gentle voice answered, "Rich folks have their troubles, too."

Surprised, Rachel asked, "What did you say?"

An elderly gentleman wearing a straw hat appeared from behind the shrubs. He held a pair of clippers in his gloved hands. "I said rich folks have their troubles, too. What's your name, young lady?"

"Rachel Grant. I live down there," Rachel answered, pointing to the small, white frame house a few doors farther down Shiloh Way. Wide-eyed with curiosity, she exclaimed, "Are *you* the Colonel?"

"Guilty as charged," the man answered. "You can call me Col. James if you like."

"Oh my goodness! You're not a mean old buzzar...I, I mean, you're a... what I'm tryin' to say is that you seem like a really nice man."

"Well, thank you, Rachel," the Colonel said with a chuckle as he snipped yellowed leaves and spent blooms from the azaleas.

"Your home's very beautiful. You must love it here. I've never seen so many pretty flowers in all my life! How do you keep everything so neat? Does anybody help you? I live just three houses down the street, and I've never even seen you. Why do you keep to yourself so much? Do you *ever* leave Shiloh? Don't you get lonesome?" Rachel asked.

"How can you ask *five* questions without even taking a breath?" the Colonel replied in jest.

"My mama says I could talk the ears off the Statue of Liberty!" Rachel said.

At that remark, the Colonel laughed loudly. It had been a long time since he'd engaged in conversation, let alone laughed, with someone.

"I get lonely," Rachel continued. "Mama has to work a lot, and I don't have any brothers or sisters."

Col. James asked, "What about your dad?"

"I don't have a daddy either. He died when I was a baby," Rachel said.

After an awkward silence, Rachel smiled and said, "Well, I better be gettin' home. I gotta do my homework. It was nice meetin' you, sir. Goodbye, Col. James."

"It was a pleasure meeting you, Miss Rachel Grant," the Colonel said. "And by the way, I do keep the grounds myself. Neatness is something I learned in the army. And if it's okay with your mama, you're welcome to come over sometime and help me tend my flowers and plant my vegetable garden."

"Really!" Rachel exclaimed. "I'd love to do that! I'll ask Mama tonight. Maybe I'll see you tomorrow. Goodbye, Col. James, and thank you!"

"Goodbye, Rachel," he said and returned to his pruning.

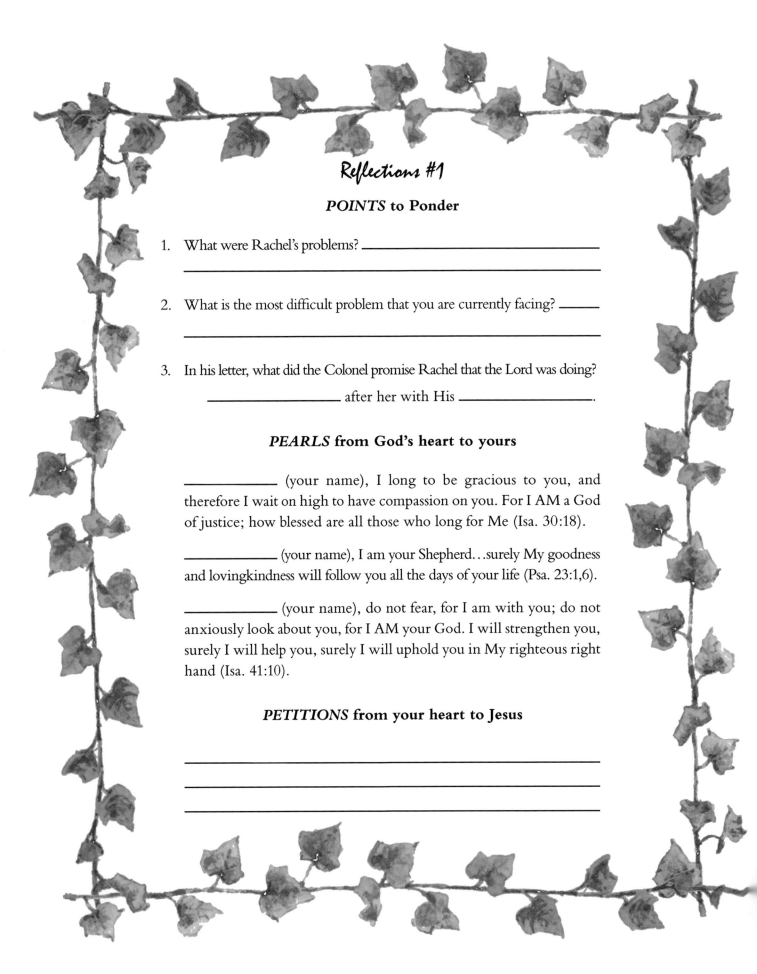

Reflections #1

POINTS to Ponder

1. What were Rachel's problems? _____
   _____

2. What is the most difficult problem that you are currently facing? _____
   _____

3. In his letter, what did the Colonel promise Rachel that the Lord was doing?
   _____ after her with His _____.

PEARLS from God's heart to yours

_____ (your name), I long to be gracious to you, and therefore I wait on high to have compassion on you. For I AM a God of justice; how blessed are all those who long for Me (Isa. 30:18).

_____ (your name), I am your Shepherd…surely My goodness and lovingkindness will follow you all the days of your life (Psa. 23:1,6).

_____ (your name), do not fear, for I am with you; do not anxiously look about you, for I AM your God. I will strengthen you, surely I will help you, surely I will uphold you in My righteous right hand (Isa. 41:10).

PETITIONS from your heart to Jesus

_____
_____
_____

Chapter 2:
An Extraordinary Friendship

The following afternoon, Rachel rushed from the bus stop to the gates of Shiloh. To her delight, she saw Col. Hamilton in the distance. He "just happened" to be picking up sticks under the oak trees when Rachel's bus arrived.

"Hi, Col. James," Rachel hollered. "Mama said I can help you in your garden. I'm goin' home to do my homework, and then I'll come right back. Is that okay?"

"That's A-Okay with me," he answered and waved. "Take your time and do your best on that school work. Anything worth doing is worth doing with excellence. That's another lesson I learned in the army."

"Yes, sir. I'll be back soon," Rachel called.

"I'll be in the rose garden. The gate's unlocked, so just come on in when you're ready," he said. After watching Rachel run all the way home, the Colonel placed the sticks he'd collected into a wheelbarrow and whistled a cheery tune as he rolled the barrow to the back of the house.

Life at Shiloh differed greatly from the forty years Col. Hamilton served in the military. After graduating from the University of Alabama in the spring of 1941, he enlisted in the U.S. Army and immediately began Officer Candidate School (OCS) at Fort Benning, Georgia. As war threatened the United States, Hamilton excelled in this fourteen-week program established to train infantry officers in preparation for combat. Just three months after he graduated with honors from OCS, the Japanese bombed Pearl Harbor, and on Dec. 8, 1941, the United States declared war. When the U.S. entered World War II, James Hamilton's life changed forever.

In less than an hour, Rachel returned to Shiloh, opened the gate, and walked down the driveway. The landscape behind those walls looked even more magnificent than the view from the street. Purple, yellow, and white pansies filled the bed surrounding an elaborate, three-tiered fountain. Large baskets overflowing with lush ferns and colorful impatiens hung between the white columns of the veranda, and deep red geraniums nestled in terracotta clay pots sat at the top and bottom of the front stairway.

She found a step-stone path that led to a small fishpond and paused to watch iridescent-orange goldfish weave gracefully in and out of their lily pad palace. A toad croaked loudly and with one hop, disappeared under a display of concentric rings dancing across the water.

Rachel followed the pathway that ended at a gazebo in the center of a lovely rose garden. Under the shelter's cedar shingled roof hung a face-to-face bench swing. Col. Hamilton stood behind the gazebo carefully pruning a pink and yellow peace rose and didn't seem to hear Rachel approaching.

"You sure do spend a lot of time cuttin' things off your trees and bushes," Rachel commented.

"Oh. Hi Rachel. Pruning the branches supports fresh, new growth by removing the damaged or dead parts. It makes the plants stronger and healthier and helps them produce more flowers and better fruit," he explained.

"We're like plants in a way," he continued. "Sometimes God prunes us back to help us grow and be fruitful. But, unfortunately, we often don't understand the value of His work until it's too late."

"Did you learn that in the army, too?" Rachel asked.

"No," the Colonel answered softly. Looking over Rachel's shoulder toward the apple orchard, he said, "Shiloh taught me that lesson."

Two lonesome hearts began to fill with a beautiful friendship on that pleasant, Alabama-April afternoon. Rachel loved following the Colonel around Shiloh and watching the old man tend to his flowers and fruit trees. He listened attentively to the young girl's chatter and patiently answered her countless questions.

When Rachel got home, she couldn't stop talking about her new friend. Bethany sat down on the edge of her daughter's canopy bed after tucking the soft comforter under Rachel's chin. "I know what we can do, Rach," she said. "Let's bake a cake for the Colonel and take it to him on Saturday. I'd like to thank him for the kindness he's shown you, and I'd also like to get to know him better."

"That's a great idea!" Rachel said. "Oh, Mama, you're gonna just love Col. James! He is *so* smart. He knows about *everything*. They must teach you a lot of stuff in the army. I think I might join the army one day. Next week, we're gonna plant his vegetable garden. Have you ever planted a garden, Mama? What kinda cake should we make? Oh, let's make him your yummy chocolate chip pound cake."

Bethany laughed and kissed Rachel's forehead, "Well, I hope the Colonel's ears are cemented on tighter than Miss Liberty's! Good night, Sugar. Don't forget to say your prayers."

For the remainder of that school year, Rachel visited Shiloh as often as her mother permitted. Dianne Fitzpatrick offered once again to keep Rachel over the summer break while Bethany worked; consequently, on many straw-hat days, Rachel and Martin ventured to Shiloh to work along side the old veteran.

"Mama, can we go back over to Shiloh after supper?" Martin asked. "Col. James said he'd help us catch lightnin' bugs tonight if it's alright with you."

Dianne glanced at her husband who grinned and nodded. "I reckon so," Dianne said. "But y'all try not to pester that poor old man to death!"

"Oh, we're not pests, Miss Dianne! I promise! We help Col. James a lot, and he says he loves for us to come visit," Rachel assured her.

When the children reached Shiloh, they saw Col. Hamilton standing near the gates holding a flashlight and three Mason jars with holes punched in the lids. The sun had already dropped below the horizon, and a waxing moon glowed in the eastern sky. Crickets and July flies played a moonlight concerto under the trees while bullfrogs croaked in perfect cadence beside the fishpond. Tiny lights blinked on and off, on and off, in all directions.

"Wow, look at all the fireflies!" Martin said.

"It looks like they're sending messages in Morse code," the Colonel observed.

"What's Morse code?" Rachel asked.

"Well, Morse code is a communication system used to send messages. Series of short dots and long dashes of light or sound represent letters of the alphabet. It was named after Samuel Finley Breese Morse – an American artist and inventor living in the 1800s. A number of inventors actually helped develop and perfect the system and the telegraph machine. But since Morse was considered the greatest advocate of telegraphy, the code was named for him," the Colonel expounded.

"Cool!" Rachel and Martin exclaimed in unison.

"Radio telegraphy became extremely valuable to us during the war. The radio transmitted calls for help, or SOS, saved many a life," the Colonel said.

"Will you show us?" Rachel begged.

"SOS looks like this," the Colonel said. Pointing his flashlight toward the children, he signaled: dot dot dot (S) dash dash dash (O) dot dot dot (S). "Radio Morse code provided long distance communication between our Navy ships, as well as, it enabled our troops to maneuver and fight more successfully."

"If you used radio signals, how did you keep the enemy from interceptin' the messages?" Martin asked.

Col. James smiled, "You're a very perceptive young man, Martin. We used encryption. In other words, the allies used code names and transformed the information we called 'plaintext' into an algorithm or 'cipher' so the enemy could neither read nor understand our messages. For example, OPERATION OVERLORD became the code name for the invasion of France, and I chose SOLOMON as my code name."

"That's just too cool! I wanna learn Morse Code," Martin said enthusiastically.

"Me, too!" Rachel agreed. "And, I think we need code names, too!"

"I'll make you kids copies of the code and start teaching it to you the next time you come over," Col. James promised. "Since Rachel means sheep in Hebrew, your code name can be 'Little Lamb'. As for you, Martin, you'll be 'Mighty Warrior' because I see great strength in you."

At that commendation, Martin stood a little straighter and lifted his chin. The Colonel handed Martin and Rachel each a jar and said, "Okay, let's see who can catch the most lightning bugs in fifteen minutes. Ready, set, go!"

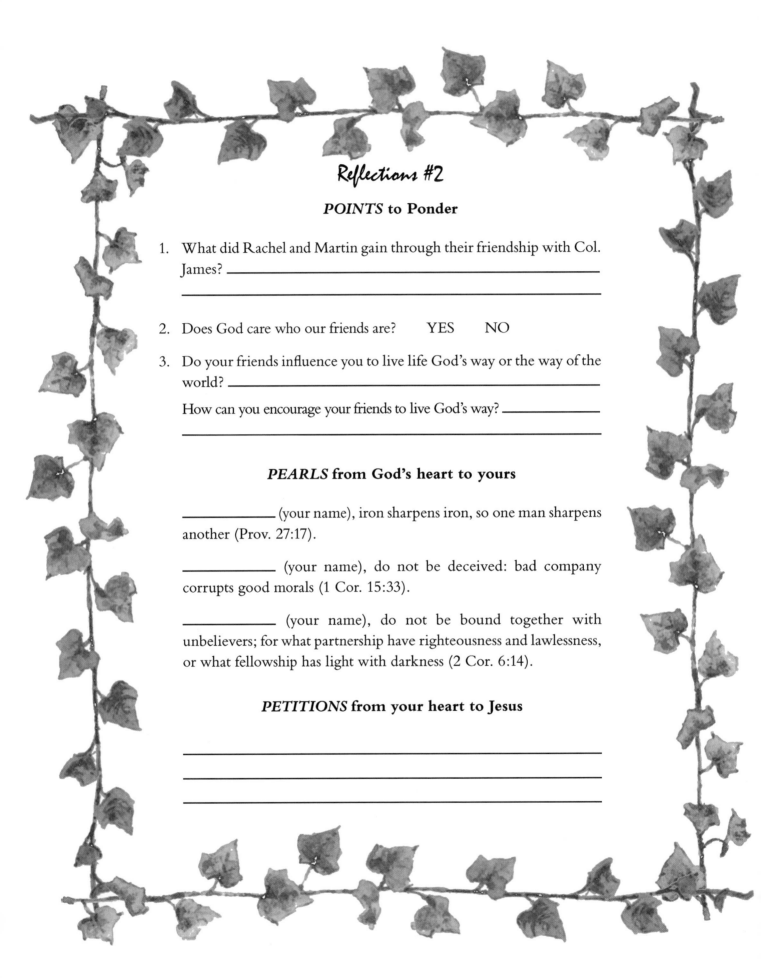

Reflections #2

POINTS to Ponder

1. What did Rachel and Martin gain through their friendship with Col. James? _____
   _____

2. Does God care who our friends are?   YES   NO

3. Do your friends influence you to live life God's way or the way of the world? _____

   How can you encourage your friends to live God's way? _____
   _____

PEARLS from God's heart to yours

_____ (your name), iron sharpens iron, so one man sharpens another (Prov. 27:17).

_____ (your name), do not be deceived: bad company corrupts good morals (1 Cor. 15:33).

_____ (your name), do not be bound together with unbelievers; for what partnership have righteousness and lawlessness, or what fellowship has light with darkness (2 Cor. 6:14).

PETITIONS from your heart to Jesus

_____

_____

_____

Chapter 3
The Key

Colonel Hamilton helped Rachel and Martin learn Morse code that summer, and he also gave them flashlights equipped with special buttons to send dot-and-dash messages. In the evenings, the Colonel created war games for the children as a fun way of teaching them problem solving and critical thinking. Through coded messages and cryptic clues, the old officer led the children on secret missions and intriguing scavenger hunts. When separated across Shiloh, SOS became the signal for the threesome to reassemble immediately.

After "mission accomplished", the children would sit on the lawn under a twinkling, night sky and listen to the Colonel tell one war story after another. They learned that in early 1942, America suffered a series of defeats in the Philippines, and the Japanese landed in New Guinea, threatening Australia. Col. James said that the tides began to turn in favor of the Allies when U.S. air units bombed Tokyo and valiantly fought in the Battle of the Coral Sea and the Battle of Midway, stopping Japan's advance in the Pacific.

"The army sent me to the South Pacific in 1943," he said. "As a young captain, I had to grow up fast. In '44, I received orders to go to France as part of one of the largest operations in history."

"Gen. Dwight D. Eisenhower commanded OPERATION OVERLORD. The assault required four thousand ships, one hundred forty thousand troops, thirteen thousand planes, and two thousand gliders. We only had a six-day window of favorable tide conditions along Normandy's shores to allow our troops to hit the beaches in darkness just before sunrise. Just two days before D-Day, heavy rains caused high waves. But, by God's mercy, the weather improved, and the mission advanced. I came ashore on Omaha Beach under the command of Gen. Omar Bradley."

The children's jaws dropped in amazement as the Colonel described his own personal account of the Normandy Invasion – D-Day, June 6, 1944.

"Germans and their machine guns were nested all along the bluff, and bullets hammered all around us. I remember how scared, but determined, I felt. Fighting was hard and casualties were high, but after numerous battles, we eventually drove the Germans inland."

Those hot, solstice days spent with Col. Hamilton included more than war stories and games. The children hoed long rows of vegetables, weeded flowerbeds, and mowed grass at Shiloh. The Colonel often loaded baskets to the brim with vine-ripened tomatoes, butter beans, yellow summer squash, cucumbers, and plump ears of silver queen corn and then sent them home with his young comrades. In all their "born days", Rachel and Martin had never worked so hard, while having so much fun.

Summertime ended all too quickly, and school days began again. Rachel soon discovered that Mary Alice Wicker's unkind remarks had not changed, but Rachel had. Time spent with her beloved Colonel had given her a new inner strength and confidence. Over the summer, she had talked to Col. James about the coming challenges of middle school, her joys, her heartaches, her dreams, and her disappointments. He listened intently and seemed to always have a word of wisdom or advice to offer her.

Col. Hamilton changed, too. Bethany insisted that the Colonel join them for Sunday dinners and worship services at Liberty Chapel. He became friends with many of the families in that congregation, as well as an admired character around Ebenezer.

Over time, the Colonel became more like Rachel's grandfather than a mere friend. Weeks rolled into months and months stretched into years. The old gentleman walked more gingerly nowadays and seemed to have a harder time keeping up the grounds of Shiloh. However, he never abandoned his three o'clock post near the iron gates to see Rachel when she got off the school bus. They both enjoyed those afternoon heart-to-hearts because their long visits together decreased as Rachel grew older and school demands increased.

One afternoon in the fall of Rachel's sophomore year of high school, the Colonel asked if she would do him the pleasure of accompanying him on a walk the following Saturday. He explained that he had some things to show her and something he'd like to tell her. She eagerly agreed, and they planned to meet at his gates Saturday morning at ten o'clock.

On Saturday, the neighborhood trees, stained in autumn gold, crimson red, and pumpkin orange, presented a striking contrast against the deep blue, October sky. Rachel zipped her jacket as she hurried to meet the Colonel. She loved the sound of dry leaves crunching under her tennis shoes as she ran toward Shiloh. Promptness was another valuable lesson her dear friend had learned in the army, and she didn't want to keep him waiting.

Their long, unhurried walk ended, to her surprise, at the cemetery behind Liberty Chapel. The Colonel opened the gate of the picket fence and said, "Did you know people are just *dying* to get in here!"

Rachel laughed and said, "Now that's funny!"

Col. James led his loyal friend to an older section of the graveyard and pointed out the headstones of his parents and grandparents. Then he suggested, "Let's go sit over there on that bench for a little while." Rachel noticed that he looked tired and rather pale, but the old warrior never complained.

"Rachel, I've shared many things with you over the years, but I regret that I've failed to share the most valuable part of my life – my relationship with God. Tough, old birds from my generation keep our faith to ourselves, and that's not good. Well, I want to change that today."

Her aging companion paused for a moment then continued, "Rachel, what you do with the time you have on this earth is very important. Did you know that God prepared special work for each of us to do while we're here?"

"No sir," Rachel answered.

"Well, He did. Ephesians 2:10 says that we are God's workmanship, created for good works, which He prepared beforehand for all of His children," the Colonel expounded. "Life is short, Little Lamb. In the book of James, the Bible says we are just like a mist that appears for a little while and then vanishes away. I regret that I got so tangled up in heartache and myself that I wasted many years that were gifts from God. Am I making sense?"

"Kinda…uh…not really," Rachel admitted.

"Well then, let me just 'shoot from the hip'. Rachel, I believe that Jesus Christ is the Son of God and that He died in my place to take the punishment for my many sins. I've gotten to know Him over the years the same way you get to know anybody – by spending time together. Everyday, I hear His voice through the Bible, and I talk to Him through prayer. As a matter of fact, I pray for you and Martin all the time, and I'm sorry that I've never even told you that. I know things have been hard for you and your mama since your dad died. But, Rachel, life is hard in some way or another for everybody. Don't become imprisoned by your problems like I was, but live in freedom by faith in God through Jesus – trusting Him in every situation. Learn to live in contentment and gratitude for whatever God gives you, and watch out for that dangerous snare of dissatisfaction."

"Yes, sir," she said softly. Col. James' serious tone made her feel uneasy – like something was wrong.

"Also, never forget that you have an enemy, the devil. He's a liar and a deceiver, and you need to learn to recognize his lies. The Good Book tells us in First Peter that he's a sly foe who prowls around like a roaring lion, seeking someone to devour and destroy. You must resist him, firm in your faith."

"Even if you don't fully understand what I'm trying to tell you today, just remember these words of advice: get to know the Lord Jesus, Rachel, and serve Him with all your heart. He's worthy to be trusted and obeyed. The Lord *will* take care of you, Rachel, and your mother. I promise. He's chasing after you with His goodness. You just have to be still and let Him catch you – and don't do all the talkin', young lady," he added with a caring smile.

After the Colonel finished his discourse, he pulled a little box from his coat pocket. Inside the box, a golden key on a delicately woven chain rested on the white satin lining. "I'd like for you to have this," he said.

"Oh, it's beautiful! Thank you, Col. James! What does the key open?" she asked as she slipped the necklace over her head.

In a rather secretive manner, he answered, "You'll figure that out when the time's right."

Both Rachel and the Colonel remained quiet on their walk home. When they reached Shiloh's gates, Rachel gave the old man a tight hug and kissed his wrinkled cheek. "Thank you for my pretty necklace. I love you, Col. James. Goodbye," she said, then turned and walked home.

The next morning, Rachel woke to the ringing doorbell. A few minutes later, her mother tapped on her bedroom door and then opened it. Bethany sat down beside Rachel and took her hand. "Pastor McKenzie came to see us," she said.

Rachel yawned and asked, "Pastor McKenzie? What was he doin' here so early?"

"He brought you this letter from the Colonel," Bethany said tenderly and then handed her an envelope. "Sweetheart, I have some sad news. Col. James passed away last night."

"You still tryin' to figure out that letter?" Martin asked.

"You startled me. What are you doin' here?" Rachel replied.

"Lookin' for you," Martin said. "Your mom's worried about you, and she called my mama. I thought you might've finally decided to come back to Shiloh, so I came lookin' for you."

Reaching for the letter, he asked, "Can I give it a shot?"

Rachel handed the letter to Martin. *I wish Col. James could see him now,* she thought. Her friend had matured considerably since that fun summer between sixth and seventh grade. Playing football the past three seasons at Ebenezer High School had added clearly defined muscles to his well over six-foot frame.

"Don't be afraid, Little Lamb." Martin read aloud. "Little Lamb…hmmm… that's the code name Col. James gave you that summer we played over here so much. Do you remember that, Rach?"

"Of course I do," she answered.

"The Lord has seen your SOS…the answer to all your troubles rests at Shiloh," he read thoughtfully. After a moment of silence, Martin yelled, "Rachel!"

"What? You scared me to death," Rachel said.

"This letter…it's encryption! I believe the Colonel left you clues for your last mission at Shiloh!"

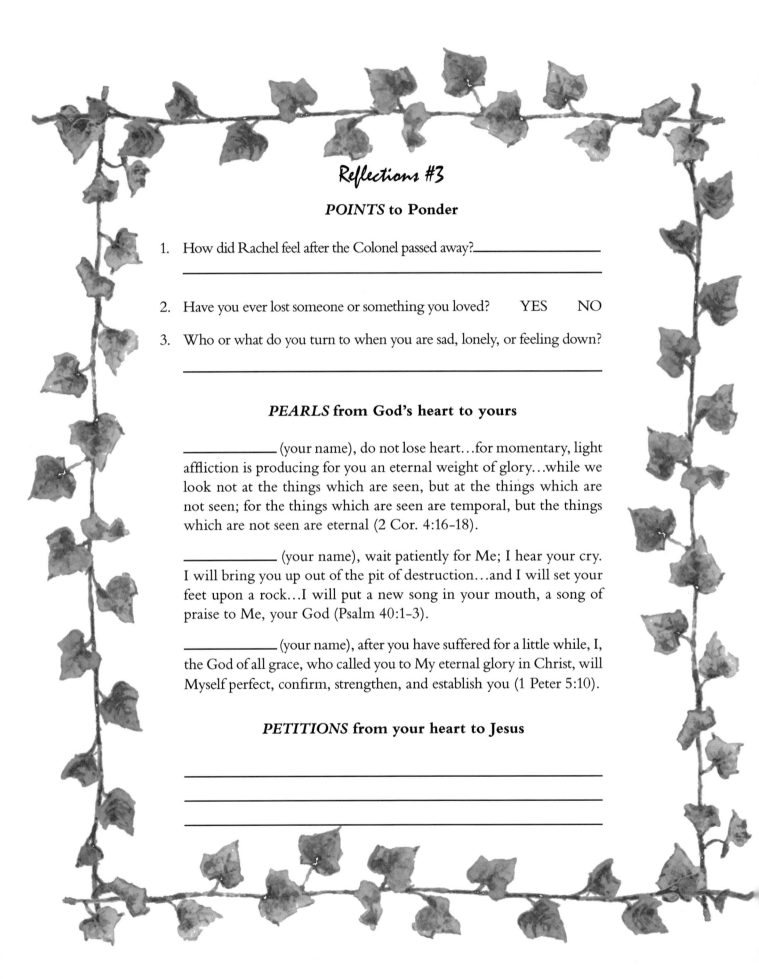

Reflections #3

POINTS to Ponder

1. How did Rachel feel after the Colonel passed away?_____
_____

2. Have you ever lost someone or something you loved?   YES   NO

3. Who or what do you turn to when you are sad, lonely, or feeling down?
_____

PEARLS from God's heart to yours

_____ (your name), do not lose heart…for momentary, light affliction is producing for you an eternal weight of glory…while we look not at the things which are seen, but at the things which are not seen; for the things which are seen are temporal, but the things which are not seen are eternal (2 Cor. 4:16-18).

_____ (your name), wait patiently for Me; I hear your cry. I will bring you up out of the pit of destruction…and I will set your feet upon a rock…I will put a new song in your mouth, a song of praise to Me, your God (Psalm 40:1-3).

_____ (your name), after you have suffered for a little while, I, the God of all grace, who called you to My eternal glory in Christ, will Myself perfect, confirm, strengthen, and establish you (1 Peter 5:10).

PETITIONS from your heart to Jesus

_____
_____
_____

Chapter 4:
Final Mission

"We'll figure it out, Rachel," Martin said. "Come on; I'll walk you home."

Martin took Rachel's hand and pulled her to her feet. Her spirits rose. Her long time friend's desire to help her surprised Rachel, because ever since they started high school, his focus on sports and other friends hadn't left much time for her.

"Tell me, again, exactly how you got that letter," Martin said as he latched the gates.

"Pastor McKenzie brought it to my house the morning after Col. James passed away," Rachel said.

"Well then, it seems to me the first thing we should do is go see Pastor McKenzie," Martin said. "He may know somethin' that will help us solve this mystery. It's four o'clock now. If we hustle, we've got time to get to the church office before it closes."

By jogging, the teens made it to Liberty Chapel in less than thirty minutes.

"Is Pastor McKenzie here, and is he busy?" Martin asked Bonnie Callahan, the church secretary.

"You know pastors only work on Sundays!" Mrs. Callahan teased. "I'm sure he has time to see you two."

"I heard that, Mrs. C.," Pastor McKenzie said in amusement as he walked out of his office. "Hi, Rachel and Martin. What brings you here today?"

Brian McKenzie had been called to pastor Liberty Chapel before Rachel and Martin were even born. Raised in Glasgow, Scotland, the young McKenzie traveled to the United States in the early 70s to attend seminary. He had planned to return to his homeland after graduation; however, a pretty, little southern bell named Margaret Eloise Hall captured the Scotsman's heart. Through his love for her, the Lord reordered his steps. Brian and Margaret married in 1977, and Liberty Chapel's need for a pastor allowed the newlyweds to settle in Alabama near her parents.

"May we talk to you, please?" Rachel asked.

"Of course. Come on in my office and have a seat," he said.

Rachel placed the letter on his desk. "I've been carryin' this letter around for over a year now. Do you have any idea what the Colonel meant?"

"When we were kids, we used to play war games with Col. James," Martin added. "I think his letter might have a hidden meaning."

Pastor McKenzie took the letter, leaned back in his chair, and carefully read over the hand-written words.

"How did you get the letter to bring it to me?" Rachel asked.

"Well, about a month before Col. Hamilton passed away, he came to see me. He seemed to know that his time to go home to God was drawing near. The Colonel asked me to give you this letter after he died. We prayed together and then he left," the pastor said. He handed the paper to Martin. "Which words do you think might be cryptic, Martin?"

"Is it okay to mark on this, Rachel?" Martin asked.

She nodded. Martin picked up a pencil and circled "Little Lamb," "SOS," and "resting at Shiloh."

Taking back the letter, the minister said, "In the Bible, Scripture often has a double meaning. For example, do you remember the story of Jonah and the whale?"

"Yes, sir," they answered.

"That experience in the Old Testament happened to an actual man; however, the story also foreshadowed an event in the life of Jesus. In Matthew 12:40, Jesus said, 'for just as Jonah was three days and three nights in the belly of the sea monster, so will the Son of Man be three days and three nights in the heart of the earth.' Jesus spoke of the time between His crucifixion and resurrection," Pastor McKenzie explained.

"All that to say, I think the word 'Shiloh' in your letter could have two meanings. Shiloh probably refers to the Colonel's home, but it could also mean…." The pastor paused, opened his Bible, and pointed to Genesis 49:10. "Read this verse for us, Rachel."

"The scepter shall not depart from Judah, nor the ruler's staff from between his feet, until *Shiloh* comes, and to him shall be the obedience of the peoples," Rachel read.

"In that verse, God promised that a king would come from the descendants of Judah. King David fulfilled that prophecy first, but Jesus Christ will ultimately fulfill it when He returns as King of kings and Lord of lords," their pastor clarified. "The name 'Shiloh', as used here, is an epithet – a word used in place of Messiah."

Pastor McKenzie looked kindheartedly at Rachel and said, "Rachel, Jesus is the Messiah. I believe the Colonel told you that the answer to all your troubles, the only real answer to anyone's problems, is Jesus."

"Yes, sir," Rachel whispered.

"Nonetheless," he added, "I also think there's most likely something somewhere at Shiloh that the Colonel wanted you to find."

Rachel appeared to be getting uncomfortable with the conversation, so Martin ended the meeting abruptly by saying, "Well, that's all the questions we have for now, Pastor. I guess we'd better be goin'. Thank you for your time."

"Yes, thank you, sir," Rachel said.

"Let me know what you find," Pastor McKenzie said. "Col. Hamilton was a good man, and I miss him. Please come back if you'd like to talk again."

After the teens left, Pastor McKenzie closed his office door and knelt down beside his desk. "Father, thank You for Rachel and Martin coming today. Lord, I confess I doubted that Col. Hamilton's plan would come to fruition. Forgive my lack of faith in You, Lord. Please guide them as they began their search. When the time is right, help them unlock the secrets of Shiloh. Give them wisdom, and by Your Holy Spirit, please draw Rachel and Martin unto Yourself. Be glorified, O Lord! I ask these things in Jesus' name. Amen and amen."

"Whatcha thinkin'?" Martin asked as the teens walked toward Shiloh Way.

Rachel sounded disappointed, "I'm still as confused as ever. Of course a preacher's gonna say that Jesus is the answer to all your problems."

Martin looked deep in thought as they strolled down Rachel's street. When they reached her house, Martin said, "Pastor McKenzie might have pointed us in the right direction, though. Remember, you said that Col. James told you that he prayed for us and read the Bible everyday? Well, if the name 'Shiloh' is in the Bible, maybe some of the other clues are too."

"You should be a detective one day, Marty," Rachel laughed. "That's an ingenious idea. But, looking for those three tiny clues in the whole entire Bible would be like looking for a needle in a haystack."

"Not really. I've got a plan. Meet me in the library during study hall tomorrow," he said. "Bye, Rach."

She replied, "Okay. See ya tomorrow."

She watched Martin walk down the sidewalk and disappear around the corner. Rachel couldn't believe her ears! Her world that had appeared so miserable only a few hours earlier now seemed hopeful and exciting.

"YES!" she shouted and then danced a little jig around her porch. *I think I'll leave my hair down tomorrow and wear my blue turtleneck,* she thought. *Martin's favorite color is blue.*

The next day, time seemed to move as slow as molasses in January. When the bell finally rang ending third period, Rachel jumped from her desk and scooted down the hallway to the library. She found Martin working at a computer. "Whatcha doin'?" she asked.

"Decipherin'," he said with a grin. "Okay, we assumed that the Colonel wrote 'Little Lamb' as a clue that code words are embedded in his letter. Since 'SOS' was the first code term he taught us, let's start there."

Martin navigated to a search website and typed in 'SOS'. "Great," he laughed. "There are over two hundred *million* possibilities."

"Try 'Bible SOS'," Rachel suggested.

"Oh, that helped a lot," he said sarcastically. "Now, there's only eight million."

"Pastor McKenzie says that seven means complete in the Bible. Try clickin' on page seven just for the fun of it and see whatcha find."

"*Oh…my…goodness,*" Martin said. "I'm not believin' this."

"What? What is it, Martin?" Rachel demanded.

"Rachel, what was Col. James' code name?"

"Solomon. Why?" she asked.

Martin looked at Rachel and said, "Remember he told us that he *chose* that code name? Well, listen to this: SOS in the Bible stands for **S**ong **O**f **S**ongs or **S**ong **O**f ***Solomon***!"

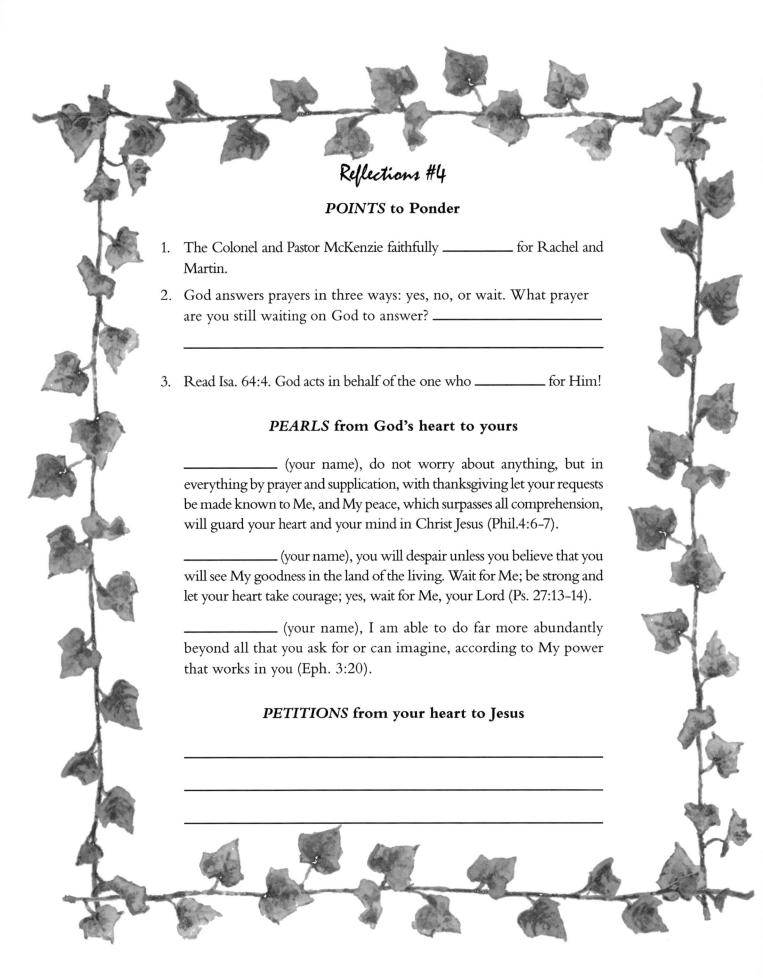

Reflections #4

POINTS to Ponder

1. The Colonel and Pastor McKenzie faithfully _____ for Rachel and Martin.

2. God answers prayers in three ways: yes, no, or wait. What prayer are you still waiting on God to answer? _____

   _____

3. Read Isa. 64:4. God acts in behalf of the one who _____ for Him!

PEARLS from God's heart to yours

_____ (your name), do not worry about anything, but in everything by prayer and supplication, with thanksgiving let your requests be made known to Me, and My peace, which surpasses all comprehension, will guard your heart and your mind in Christ Jesus (Phil.4:6-7).

_____ (your name), you will despair unless you believe that you will see My goodness in the land of the living. Wait for Me; be strong and let your heart take courage; yes, wait for Me, your Lord (Ps. 27:13-14).

_____ (your name), I am able to do far more abundantly beyond all that you ask for or can imagine, according to My power that works in you (Eph. 3:20).

PETITIONS from your heart to Jesus

_____

_____

_____

Chapter 5
Solomon's Song

That night, Rachel hunted through the books on her bedroom shelves until she found the Bible her grandmother Grant had given her on her eighth birthday. She snuggled under the covers and opened her neglected book to the table of contents. "Song of Solomon, where is Song of Solomon?" she said. "Ah, of course, here it is – right between Ecclesi…something-or-other and Isaiah."

Turning to Chapter One, she read: "The Song of Songs which is Solomon's. May he kiss me with the kisses of his mouth! For your love is better than wine."

"Woe! This is a love song! I didn't know the Bible had stories like this. I don't think we'll find *anything* related to Col. James in *this* book of the Bible!" Rachel laughed. "But I promised Martin I'd read Chapter One tonight. So how many chapters are there anyway? Let me see…eight chapters. Okay, here we go."

Rachel had just finished reading when the phone rang. "Hello," she said. "Oh. Hi Martin."

"I've got another idea! Since Pastor McKenzie thinks there's something at Shiloh that the Colonel wanted you to find, let's clean up the place and see what we uncover. Football spring training doesn't start until the end of April, so I'll have some extra time until then. Whatcha think?" Martin asked eagerly.

"Sounds good to me," Rachel said. "Martin, why are you doing all this anyway? I mean, we haven't really hung out together since middle school."

"Well, I really thought a lot of Col. James, and I've just gotta figure out what his letter means. It's drivin' me crazy!" Martin said. "Besides, I know it's important to you, and friends should be there for each other. So, can you meet me Saturday morning at the gates?"

"Sure. What time?" Rachel asked.

"Nine o'clock sharp!" Martin said. "G'night."

On Saturday, Martin drove up to the entrance of Shiloh in his dad's truck just as Rachel arrived by foot. "Do you think we'll be able to get in the shed to get some tools?" Rachel asked.

"I brought a couple of rakes and a tarp just in case it's locked," Martin answered. "Mom also gave me a box of giant trash bags to put the leaves in."

The old tool shed sat about fifty yards away from the apple orchard. They found the shed unlocked, and Martin opened the door. The two friends peered inside. A wave of memories swept over Rachel and Martin as they looked at the rakes, hoes, and shovels hanging in a straight row along the back wall like soldiers on the front battle line. Except for cobwebs and a musty smell, nothing had changed. The Colonel's workbench in the back corner sat well ordered with every nail, hammer, and screwdriver in its place, and his frayed straw hat and dirty work gloves still hung on two rusty hooks by the door.

Rachel took a rake from the wall and said, "Let's start in the rose garden."

They walked to the deserted garden and began clearing sticks and leaves from around the bushes.

"So tell me, what'ya think about Song of Solomon?" Rachel asked Martin as she helped him rake a large pile of leaves onto the tarpaulin.

"Not what I expected," he snickered. "But I'm not givin' up. Let's keep readin' a chapter a night, and maybe we'll find somethin' connected to your letter."

After three hours of raking, pulling weeds, and bagging piles of debris, the friends decided to call it a day. "Maybe we can come back next week after school," Martin said. "I'll see you tomorrow at church."

"Sounds good. Wanna sit in our old spot from middle school?" Rachel suggested.

The following morning, Pastor McKenzie smiled when he saw Rachel and Martin sitting together on the front pew during the worship service. After the closing benediction, the pastor called to them as the congregation exited the auditorium, "How's your hunt coming along?"

"We think we've found a lead for one of the clues," Martin said. "Since you showed us that 'Shiloh' is in the Bible, we looked up 'SOS' and found the book of Song of Solomon. Did you know Col. James' code name in World War II was Solomon?"

"Bonny good work, lad!" the pastor said and grinned broadly.

"We also decided to clean up the grounds of Shiloh," Rachel added.

"I have great confidence in you two! You'll solve this mystery yet," their pastor encouraged. "God bless you, children."

February soon ended, and that South Alabama March tiptoed in more like a lamb instead of the proverbial roaring lion. Yellow crocuses poked their heads above ground, announcing the coming of springtime, and the red bud trees, waking from another winter's nap, opened their lavender eyes. Sprouting leaves on the hardwood branches gave a fresh, green welcome to the landscape stirring from hibernation.

Martin and Rachel used every minute they could spare to refurbish the grounds of Shiloh. Unbeknownst to Rachel, Martin turned down an invitation to a spring break beach trip, so that Rachel wouldn't have to work alone.

"I've read all the way through Song of Solomon three times and I don't see any connection between that book and the Colonel," Martin remarked one afternoon as he and Rachel picked up limbs under the oak trees along Shiloh's driveway.

"Yeah, it's kinda hard to understand," Rachel said. "This place is startin' to look pretty good. The Colonel would be pleased, don't ya think?"

Martin replied, "Yep, I think he would. Anyway, I finally figured out that Solomon's song is a conversation between King Solomon and his bride."

"Yeah. My favorite part of the book is Chapter Two. It reminds me of Shiloh," Rachel said.

"What did you say?" Martin asked.

"I said Chapter Two sound like a description of Shi…loh. Wait a minute. Are you thinkin' what I'm thinkin'?" Rachel asked.

"I've got my Bible in the truck," Martin said. "I'll be right back."

Martin quickly returned carrying his Bible. "Let's go sit in the gazebo," he suggested.

Facing Rachel, Martin said, "Show me every verse you think describes Shiloh."

Rachel opened the leather Bible to Song of Solomon Chapter Two. "Let's see," she said as she studied the passage. "Well, first of all, verse one talks about the rose of Sharon and the lilies. Shiloh has both kinds of those flowers. Uh…verse nine refers to lattice windows, and the kitchen windows of the mansion are lattice. And, for heaven's sake, verses eleven and twelve could've been written today: 'For behold, the winter is past, the rain is over and gone. The flowers have already appeared in the land; the time has arrived for pruning the vines, and the voice of the turtle dove has been heard in our land.'"

Martin put his hand on her shoulder and asked, "Rachel, verse three talks about an apple tree, and Shiloh has a whole apple orchard. Why did you skip that passage?" And then he read, "Like an apple tree among the trees of the forest, so is my beloved among the young men."

Her chin quivered and a single tear rolled down her cheek. "Oh Martin. You know why I skipped that verse. It reminds me of Col. James' funeral. After the service that day, when Pastor McKenzie told us the Colonel had requested a *private* burial in the apple orchard at Shiloh, it was just easier to never go to the orchard – to never see his grave."

Martin took Rachel's hand and said, "Come on. We'll go see it together."

Martin helped Rachel out of the swing and picked up their rakes. His support gave her courage, and the couple walked hand-in-hand to the back of the apple orchard.

Under the fruit trees, they found a simple, marble headstone that read:

COL. JAMES BEAUREGARD HAMILTON

ALABAMA

U.S. ARMY

WORLD WAR II

DECEMBER 23, 1919 - OCTOBER 8, 1997

Martin handed Rachel her rake. In reverent quietness, they worked together, clearing the fallen leaves from their old friend's resting place and the surrounding area. A few feet to the right of Col. James' marker, the teeth of Rachel's rake unexpectedly scraped across what sounded like a rock. Another stroke of the rake uncovered a weathered stone, lying flat along the ground, engraved with the image of a dove. Getting down on her hands and knees, she gently brushed away the remaining leaves and twigs and then gasped. Putting both hands to her mouth, she said, "Martin! Come here, quick, and look at this!"

Peering over Rachel's shoulder, he read:

ABIGAIL LAWRENCE HAMILTON

BELOVED WIFE OF CAPT. JAMES B. HAMILTON

APRIL 21, 1920 - JUNE 20, 1944

SONG OF SOLOMON 2:14-16

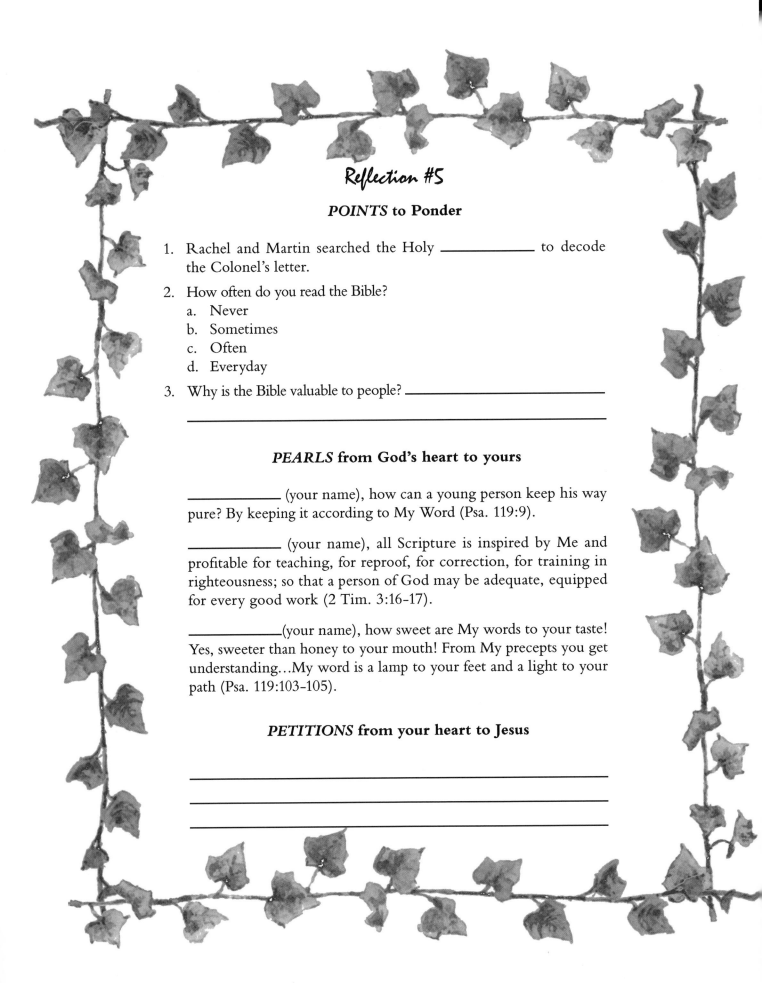

Reflection #5

POINTS to Ponder

1. Rachel and Martin searched the Holy _____ to decode the Colonel's letter.

2. How often do you read the Bible?
   a. Never
   b. Sometimes
   c. Often
   d. Everyday

3. Why is the Bible valuable to people? _____
   _____

PEARLS from God's heart to yours

_____ (your name), how can a young person keep his way pure? By keeping it according to My Word (Psa. 119:9).

_____ (your name), all Scripture is inspired by Me and profitable for teaching, for reproof, for correction, for training in righteousness; so that a person of God may be adequate, equipped for every good work (2 Tim. 3:16-17).

_____(your name), how sweet are My words to your taste! Yes, sweeter than honey to your mouth! From My precepts you get understanding...My word is a lamp to your feet and a light to your path (Psa. 119:103-105).

PETITIONS from your heart to Jesus

_____

_____

_____

Chapter 6:
Shiloh's Secret

"Martin!" Rachel said. "He was *married*!"

"Look at the date she died," Martin said. "June 20, 1944, just a couple of weeks after the Normandy Invasion – while Col. James fought in France."

"And look at the Scripture! You were right. 'SOS' *does* mean Song of Solomon," Rachel said. "He said the answer to all my problems *rests* at Shiloh. Since his wife's resting place is Shiloh, do you think those verses hold our next clue?"

"Let's go see Pastor McKenzie!" Martin said. He gathered up the rakes and grabbed Rachel's hand again. They sprinted to the truck parked in the driveway and drove to the church.

Pastor McKenzie was locking the outside door of the church office when they reached Liberty Chapel. Hopping from the truck, the two teenagers rushed to their pastor. "You'll never believe what we found!" they said together.

"Abigail's grave?" Pastor McKenzie asked.

"How did you know?" Rachel asked.

"When Col. Hamilton gave me your letter, Rachel, he also gave me instructions for his private burial. He asked me to place his grave beside his beloved wife," the pastor said. "Let's go inside where we can talk."

Martin carried his Bible into Pastor McKenzie's office and said, "The Scripture on her tombstone is Song of Solomon 2:14-16. We believe those verses may hold our next clue. Verse fourteen talks about 'the *secret* place of the steep pathway.'"

"But all the paths at Shiloh are flat, not steep," Rachel commented.

"Don't forget that her tombstone was engraved in 1944," the pastor reminded them. "What translation of the Bible do you have, Martin?"

"NASB," Martin answered. "Why?"

"The people of Ebenezer in that day would have used the King James Version. Let's see how it reads." Pastor McKenzie pulled a King James Bible from the shelf of his library and handed it to Rachel. "Find that verse for us, please Rachel."

Rachel opened the Bible right to Song of Solomon, found Chapter Two verse fourteen, and read, "O my dove, that art in the cleft of the rock, in the secret places of the *stairs*...."

"The front steps of the house at Shiloh are stone! There must be something hidden in those stairs. It's gettin' too dark to go look now, but tomorrow's Saturday. We can start searchin' first thing in the mornin'. Wanna come with us, Pastor?" Martin asked.

"I'd love to," Pastor McKenzie said. "I'll see you first thing in the morning."

The threesome met at the gates early the next day. An aura of expectancy inundated the crisp, spring morning. Sunrays passing through the oak branches and striking the freshly mown lawn created a sparkling, green sea of dewdrop-diamonds. Martin opened the gate for Rachel and the pastor to enter first. Pastor McKenzie hummed the old hymn "In the Garden" as they walked down the drive toward the mansion.

Martin took charge, "Rachel, why don't you start at the top of the steps and work down? Pastor, we'll start at the bottom and work up – you take the left side and I'll take the right."

He's a natural born sergeant, Pastor McKenzie thought to himself.

"Martin, what exactly are we looking for?" Rachel asked.

"Some kind of secret compartment or loose stone where Col. James could've hidden somethin'," Martin answered.

They searched meticulously for about half an hour to no avail. "I can't find anything," Rachel said.

"Read that verse again, Rachel," Pastor McKenzie suggested.

"O my dove, that art in the cleft of the rock, in the secret places of the stair," Rachel read.

"In the *cleft*...maybe it's not a loose stone. Maybe there's somethin' in the cracks. Okay, let's look in every nook and cranny," Martin ordered. Rachel darted back to the top of the steps while Martin and the pastor crawled along the bottom checking the crevices.

After hunting for several more minutes, Rachel shouted in excitement, "I found somethin'!" On the far right side of the third step from the top, Rachel tried to dislodge something brown from a crack between two of the stones. "It's stuck," she said.

"Be careful; don't tear it," Martin cautioned.

On hands and knees, Rachel pinched one corner of the concealed object between her thumb and forefinger. Gently wiggling it back and forth, back and forth, she eventually pulled out a letter-sized oilcloth and sat back on her heels.

"Open it!" Martin said. He and Pastor McKenzie sat down beside Rachel and watched with anticipation as she carefully unwrapped the waterproof packaging to discover a folded piece of paper –yellowed with age. She unfolded the paper and read:

September 10, 1997

Dear Rachel and Martin,

Well done, kids! If you're reading this letter, then you've deciphered most of my first letter to Rachel and have found my darling Abigail's gravestone.

You probably have many questions. Yes, I was married to the most beautiful woman on earth - lovely in both appearance and heart. She had been gone seven weeks before I received, on the battlefields of France, the sad news of her death from tuberculosis. My heart broke. I decided that very day to bury my pain in the military, and for many years, I turned my back on God.

Rachel, on that spring afternoon in 1994 when I heard your sweet voice by Shiloh's front gates, the wall I had built around my heart and guarded for so long cracked. I believe the Lord had stood by me, patiently waiting all those years for the tiniest opening to pour life and His love back into my spirit. I thank God for the two of you, Rachel and Martin. You were God's grace-gifts to a stubborn, old man and vessels He used to bring me back to Him.

Your mission isn't over, kids. You have yet to discover the ultimate answer to all the challenges in your young lives and to learn the purpose for the key on Rachel's necklace. Therefore, your next assignment, should you choose to complete it, is to study the life of Solomon in the Holy Scriptures. Pastor McKenzie has kindly agreed to meet with you weekly as you seek to unlock the secrets of Shiloh.

I love you,

Col. James

Rachel wiped the tears running down her cheeks, and when Martin tried to speak, a lump in his throat blocked the words. "I'm sure you two have a lot to talk about," Pastor McKenzie said kindly. "I think I'll head on home. By the way, if you'd like to meet next week, Wednesday afternoon at four o'clock is a good time for me."

"Yes, sir. Thank you," Rachel managed to answer.

"One more thing," the pastor added. "A Bible concordance would be a helpful tool in your study of Solomon. I have a couple of extra ones that you may use. I'll give them to you at church in the morning."

Rachel and Martin gladly accepted the concordances from their minister. They began studying the Old Testament accounts of Solomon like they were preparing for a final exam and met daily during study hall to compare notes and discuss facts they uncovered.

After school the following Wednesday, Martin and Rachel sat across the desk from Pastor McKenzie. "What have you learned so far?" he asked.

"Well, we learned that King David was Solomon's father and that Solomon reigned as king over all Israel for forty years. We also found that there are a bazillion verses about him in the Old Testament," Martin said with a laugh.

"We discovered that he wrote two of the Psalms and many of the Proverbs. He also authored the books of Ecclesiastes and Song of Solomon, of course," Rachel added. "But we haven't come close to figurin' out the link between Solomon and my key."

"Keep digging, children, and you will," Pastor McKenzie encouraged.

Martin gave Rachel a ride home after they left the church. Gazing out the window, Rachel said, "Spring's my favorite time of the year."

"Yeah. Only a few more weeks till football practice starts," Martin said. "That's hard to believe."

"I guess you won't have much time for Solomon and me after that," Rachel said and gave Martin a weak smile.

"Yep, I'll be pretty busy, but I was wonderin'...I mean, I've been thinkin'. If you haven't already made plans...and if you want to...uh...Rachel, do you wanna go with me to the junior-senior prom in May...just as friends?" Martin stammered.

Rachel's heart pounded, but she tried to act composed. "Sure," she answered. "Sounds fun."

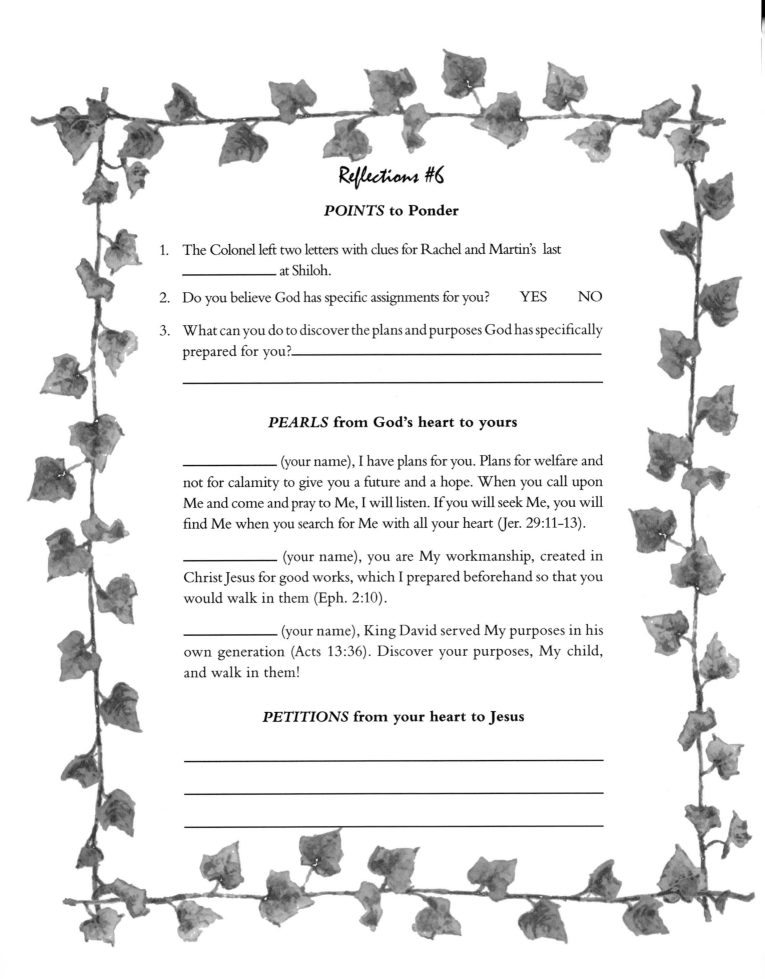

Reflections #6

POINTS to Ponder

1. The Colonel left two letters with clues for Rachel and Martin's last _____ at Shiloh.

2. Do you believe God has specific assignments for you?   YES   NO

3. What can you do to discover the plans and purposes God has specifically prepared for you?_____

_____

PEARLS from God's heart to yours

_____ (your name), I have plans for you. Plans for welfare and not for calamity to give you a future and a hope. When you call upon Me and come and pray to Me, I will listen. If you will seek Me, you will find Me when you search for Me with all your heart (Jer. 29:11-13).

_____ (your name), you are My workmanship, created in Christ Jesus for good works, which I prepared beforehand so that you would walk in them (Eph. 2:10).

_____ (your name), King David served My purposes in his own generation (Acts 13:36). Discover your purposes, My child, and walk in them!

PETITIONS from your heart to Jesus

_____

_____

_____

Chapter 7

Rachel's Shiloh

*I*n the remaining weeks before spring training, the friends worked relentlessly on the grounds of Shiloh, met with Pastor McKenzie after school, and diligently studied their Bibles. Martin organized a Scripture reading schedule for the two of them, which ended with the book of Ecclesiastes the week before football practice began.

On the day of their final reading assignment, Martin looked at Rachel across the library table and said, "Today's the last chapter of Ecclesiastes. Do you think we'll find the meanin' of your key?"

"Maybe. But even if we don't figure it out, we've learned a lot of good lessons from Solomon. It's really sad to me, though," Rachel said, "how King Solomon began his reign so strong, but then wandered away from God and got so messed up. Ecclesiastes 2:17 says he wound up hatin' life and believin' that all his work was meaningless."

"Yep, he was the wisest guy on earth and still botched things," Martin said and then picked up his books. "Well, I gotta go talk to Coach before my next class. I'll meet you at Pastor McKenzie's office after school. Bye, Rach."

"Okay. See ya, Martin," Rachel answered.

Once Martin had left, she took her Bible out of her backpack, turned to Ecclesiastes, and read all of Chapter Twelve. Closing her Bible, Rachel sat back in her chair and pulled the fine chain out from beneath her blouse. Gripping the small key tightly in her hand, she closed her eyes and whispered, "That's it! I found it, Col. James. I finally understand!"

After school, Rachel walked to the church and waited in the sanctuary until time for the meeting with Pastor McKenzie. Since childhood, the tall, stained glass window behind the right end of the altar had captivated her because, regardless of where she stood in that little chapel, Jesus's searching eyes always seemed to look deeply into hers.

She ambled toward the window and read aloud the Scripture imprinted underneath the glass masterpiece, "Behold, I stand at the door and knock; if anyone hears My voice and opens the door, I will come in to him and will dine with him, and he with Me (Revelation 3:20)."

Donny Finkleganis

The afternoon sunlight emblazed the ruby robe shrouding the Lord Jesus, as He stood, with staff in hand, knocking on the heavy, closed door. Rachel studied the detailed image of Christ's face and felt swaddled in the Savior's peace.

A few minutes before four o'clock, she made her way to Mrs. Callahan's office and found both her pastor and her best friend waiting for her. "Here she is," Pastor McKenzie said, greeting her with a fatherly hug. "Come on in, children, and have a seat."

Pastor McKenzie sat down in the chair behind his desk and asked, "Any new discoveries?"

"I found it," Rachel answered confidently. "I believe I know the meanin' of my key."

"You *did*? You *do*?" Martin asked in amazement.

Rachel opened her Bible and read Ecclesiastes 12:13, "The conclusion, when all has been heard is: fear God and keep His commandments, because this applies to every person."

"Pastor McKenzie, at our first meetin', you told us that 'Shiloh' in the book of Genesis is referrin' to the Messiah, Jesus Christ. You told us that Jesus is ultimately the answer to all our problems. I wasn't ready to accept that answer then, but after all these weeks of searchin', I've come full circle. I understand, now, what Solomon taught in the book of Ecclesiastes and what the Colonel wanted us to find. I think the lesson we're supposed to learn is that true happiness apart from Jesus is impossible," Rachel said. "I've believed that Jesus is God's Son as long as I can remember, but I haven't really known Him. I'd never surrendered my life to Jesus or had a real friendship with Him until… well, until today. I went in the chapel after school and asked Jesus to forgive my sins. I asked Him to save me from the punishment for those sins and be my Lord."

Pastor McKenzie cleared his throat and said, "Rachel, that's wonderful. I tell you the angels in heaven are rejoicing over your salvation right now! Martin, what are your thoughts?"

"Well, I've gotta admit that I started this whole thing just to help Rachel, but I've been helped, too. Jesus saved me a couple of years ago, but I've kinda been ignorin' Him. Over the past few weeks, God's shown me that I need to read the Bible and spend time with Him every day. I really wanna know the plans *He* has for me, so that I won't live a meaningless and wasted life."

"Well done, Rachel and Martin, well done!" Pastor McKenzie said proudly. "Solomon's father David instructed him in 1 Chronicles 28:9 to know God and serve Him with a whole heart and willing mind. A true *relationship* with Jesus is undeniably the real key to life!"

"So, I guess my key just opened our hearts and nothin' else," Rachel surmised.

"You both need to come with me," the pastor said. "The time has come for me to carry out *my* last mission from Col. Hamilton. Mrs. Callahan, I'll be back in about thirty or forty minutes. Do you think you can hold down the fort while I'm gone?"

"Can I? Mister, I *ran* this fort while you were still in nickers," she bantered.

Pastor McKenzie guided the teenagers three blocks down the street and stopped in front of the Ebenezer Community Bank. "After you," he said, as he held the door open for Rachel and Martin to walk in.

"What's goin' on?" Rachel whispered to Martin.

"No clue," he replied.

"Good afternoon, Mr. Peterson," the clergyman said to a gentleman in a grey suit standing behind the counter. "Will you please bring us safety deposit box number two hundred fourteen?"

Mr. Peterson led the trio into a private room, left, and then returned shortly carrying a long box with a keyhole in the top.

"Rachel, use that key on your necklace to open this box, please," Pastor McKenzie instructed.

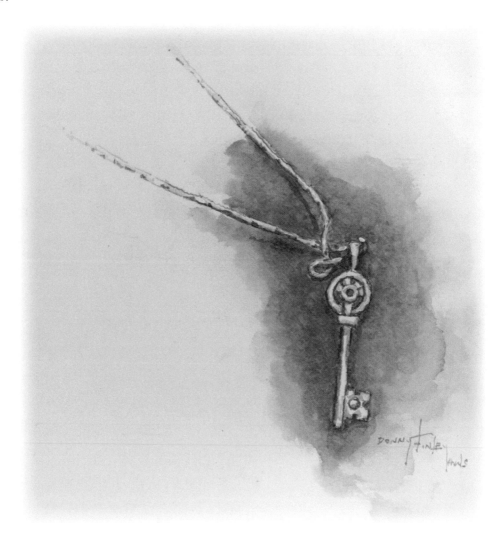

September 11, 2000

Dear Martin,

I'm counting down the days till the 24th when you graduate at Parris Island and become an official United States Marine! I'm <u>so</u> proud of you! I pray for you everyday and ask the Lord to give you the strength, endurance, and resolve to do the hard and valuable work He has set before you.

Everything's good here at school. I'm very grateful to God that the trust fund the Colonel left us enabled me to go to a Christian university. I'm studying hard and making new friends. I wish you were here!!! But I know the Colonel would be awfully proud of you for choosing to serve our country before going to college.

I have a really nice roommate from Georgia named Susan. We actually have two classes together: English 101 and Old Testament. She's helping me with English Lit, and I'm helping her in Old Testament. All that Bible study you and I did together our senior year is paying off!

Mom says the renovations at Shiloh are going well. It will be an amazing children's center for Ebenezer. She said that Pastor McKenzie has found a director and is now interviewing counselors for the staff. It's wonderful to know that kids will be blessed at that special place like you and I were. I'm just sorry that Liberty Chapel had to wait a year and a half for me - for us rather - to decipher the Colonel's letter and find the deed he left the church in his safety deposit box.

I've learned that the Hebrew name 'Shiloh' means 'His gift'. Jesus, the Shiloh, truly is God's greatest gift to mankind! The Colonel and Pastor McKenzie were right. The answer to all our troubles certainly did, do, and always will rest in the arms of our Shiloh. For Jesus Himself said: "I will never desert you, nor will I ever forsake you, so that we confidently say, the Lord is my Helper, I will not be afraid" (Hebrews 13:5b-6a). Jesus also said: "These things I have spoken to you, so that in Me you may have peace. In the world you have tribulation, but take courage; I have overcome the world" (John 16:33).

Persevere, my beloved Martin, and stay strong! May the Lord bless you and keep you; may He make His face shine on you, and be gracious to you; may the Lord lift up His countenance upon you, and give you peace (Numbers 6:24-26).

Martin, I miss you very, very much and think about you all the time. May the Lord watch between you and me while we are absent one from another (Genesis 31:49).

All my love,

Your Rachel

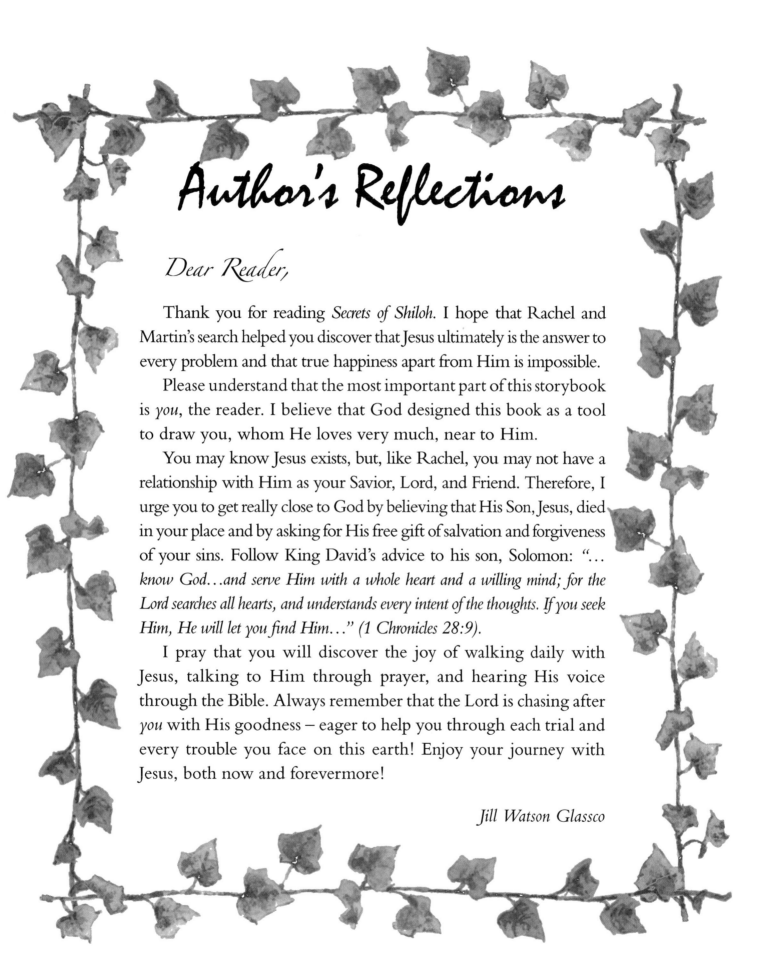

Author's Reflections

Dear Reader,

Thank you for reading *Secrets of Shiloh*. I hope that Rachel and Martin's search helped you discover that Jesus ultimately is the answer to every problem and that true happiness apart from Him is impossible.

Please understand that the most important part of this storybook is *you*, the reader. I believe that God designed this book as a tool to draw you, whom He loves very much, near to Him.

You may know Jesus exists, but, like Rachel, you may not have a relationship with Him as your Savior, Lord, and Friend. Therefore, I urge you to get really close to God by believing that His Son, Jesus, died in your place and by asking for His free gift of salvation and forgiveness of your sins. Follow King David's advice to his son, Solomon: *"…know God…and serve Him with a whole heart and a willing mind; for the Lord searches all hearts, and understands every intent of the thoughts. If you seek Him, He will let you find Him…" (1 Chronicles 28:9).*

I pray that you will discover the joy of walking daily with Jesus, talking to Him through prayer, and hearing His voice through the Bible. Always remember that the Lord is chasing after *you* with His goodness – eager to help you through each trial and every trouble you face on this earth! Enjoy your journey with Jesus, both now and forevermore!

Jill Watson Glassco

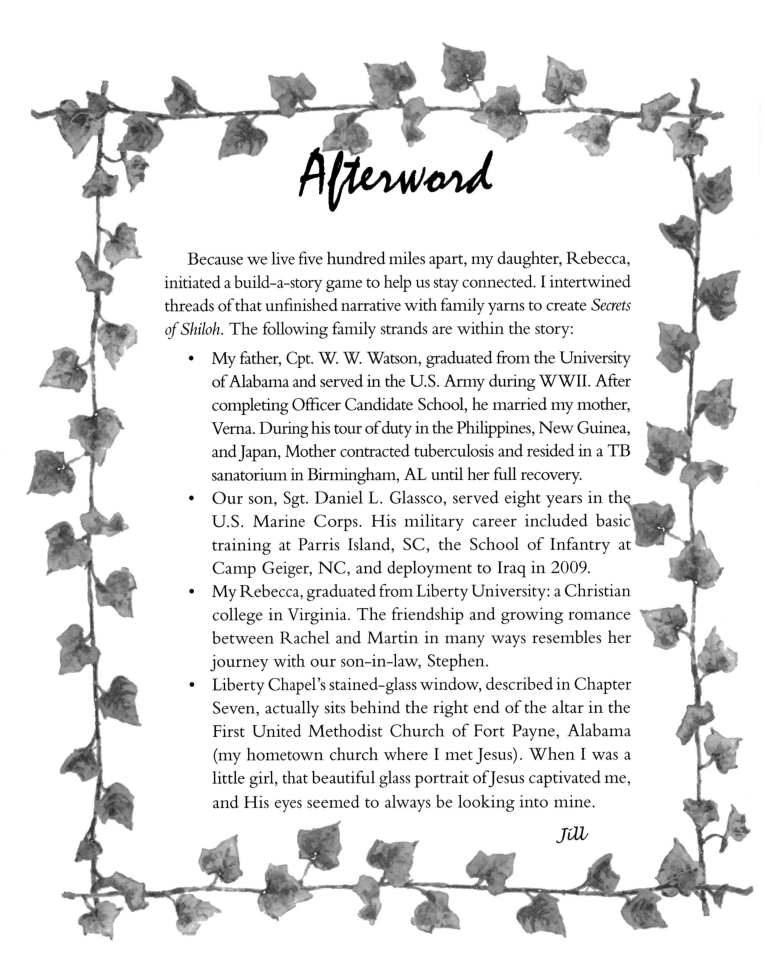

Afterword

Because we live five hundred miles apart, my daughter, Rebecca, initiated a build-a-story game to help us stay connected. I intertwined threads of that unfinished narrative with family yarns to create *Secrets of Shiloh*. The following family strands are within the story:

- My father, Cpt. W. W. Watson, graduated from the University of Alabama and served in the U.S. Army during WWII. After completing Officer Candidate School, he married my mother, Verna. During his tour of duty in the Philippines, New Guinea, and Japan, Mother contracted tuberculosis and resided in a TB sanatorium in Birmingham, AL until her full recovery.

- Our son, Sgt. Daniel L. Glassco, served eight years in the U.S. Marine Corps. His military career included basic training at Parris Island, SC, the School of Infantry at Camp Geiger, NC, and deployment to Iraq in 2009.

- My Rebecca, graduated from Liberty University: a Christian college in Virginia. The friendship and growing romance between Rachel and Martin in many ways resembles her journey with our son-in-law, Stephen.

- Liberty Chapel's stained-glass window, described in Chapter Seven, actually sits behind the right end of the altar in the First United Methodist Church of Fort Payne, Alabama (my hometown church where I met Jesus). When I was a little girl, that beautiful glass portrait of Jesus captivated me, and His eyes seemed to always be looking into mine.

Jill

CPSIA information can be obtained
at www.ICGtesting.com
Printed in the USA
LVIC07n1217100813
347244LV00003B

* 9 7 8 1 4 9 0 8 0 3 5 0 0 *